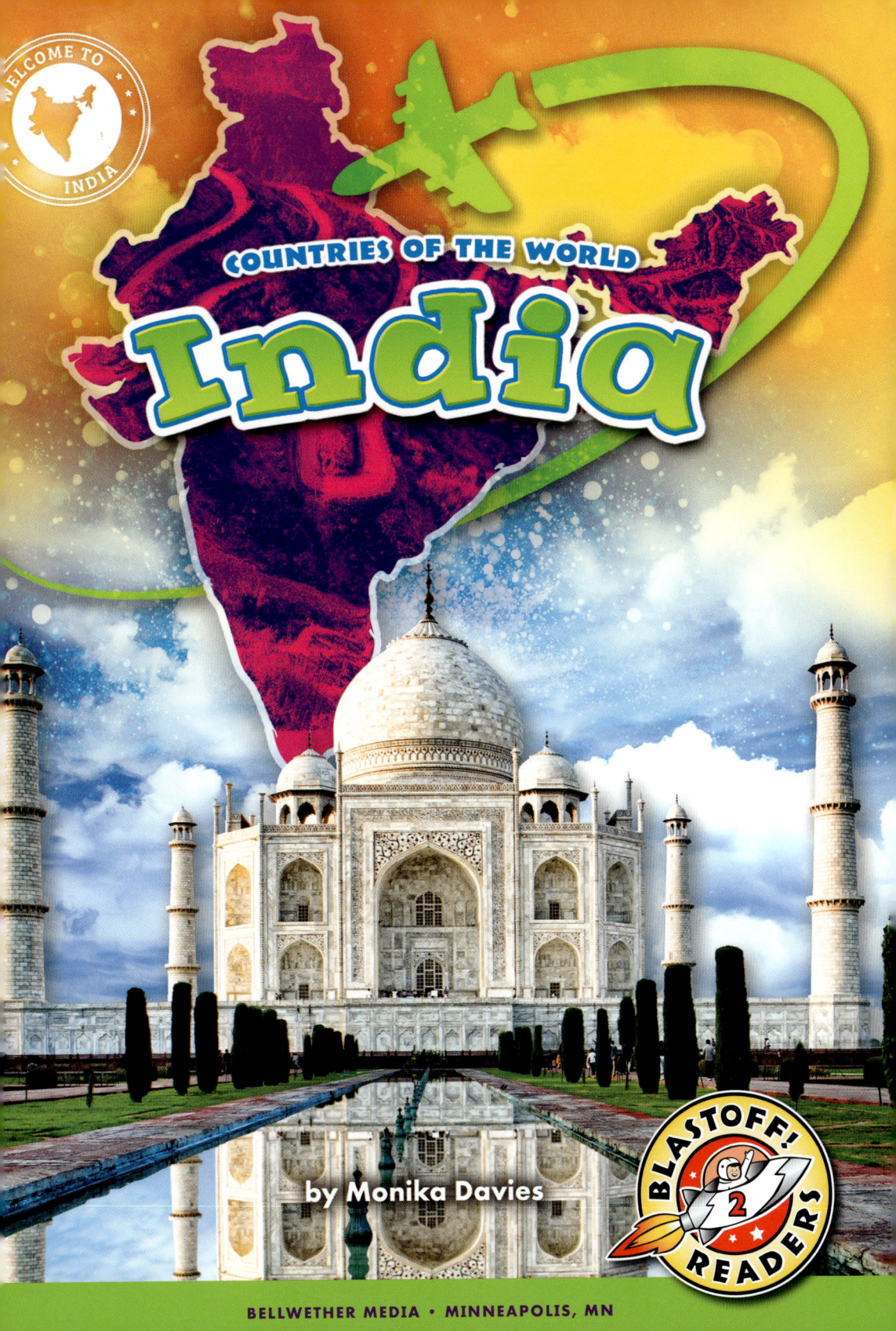

Blastoff! Readers are carefully developed by literacy experts to build reading stamina and move students toward fluency by combining standards-based content with developmentally appropriate text.

LEVELS

Level 1 provides the most support through repetition of high-frequency words, light text, predictable sentence patterns, and strong visual support.

Level 2 offers early readers a bit more challenge through varied sentences, increased text load, and text-supportive special features.

Level 3 advances early-fluent readers toward fluency through increased text load, less reliance on photos, advancing concepts, longer sentences, and more complex special features.

★ **Blastoff! Universe**

Reading Level

Grade K → Grades 1–3

→ Grade 4

This edition first published in 2023 by Bellwether Media, Inc.

No part of this publication may be reproduced in whole or in part without written permission of the publisher. For information regarding permission, write to Bellwether Media, Inc., Attention: Permissions Department, 6012 Blue Circle Drive, Minnetonka, MN 55343.

Library of Congress Cataloging-in-Publication Data

Names: Davies, Monika, author.
Title: India / by Monika Davies.
Description: Minneapolis, MN : Bellwether Media, 2023. | Series: Blastoff! Readers: Countries of the world | Includes bibliographical references and index. | Audience: Ages 5-8 | Audience: Grades 2-3 | Summary: "Relevant images match informative text in this introduction to India. Intended for students in kindergarten through third grade"– Provided by publisher.
Identifiers: LCCN 2022018168 (print) | LCCN 2022018169 (ebook) | ISBN 9781644877197 (library binding) | ISBN 9781648347658 (ebook)
Subjects: LCSH: India–Juvenile literature.
Classification: LCC DS407 .D38 2023 (print) | LCC DS407 (ebook) | DDC 954–dc23/eng/20220414
LC record available at https://lccn.loc.gov/2022018168
LC ebook record available at https://lccn.loc.gov/2022018169

Text copyright © 2023 by Bellwether Media, Inc. BLASTOFF! READERS and associated logos are trademarks and/or registered trademarks of Bellwether Media, Inc.

Editor: Elizabeth Neuenfeldt   Designer: Gabriel Hilger

Printed in the United States of America, North Mankato, MN.

Table of Contents

All About India	4
Land and Animals	6
Life in India	12
India Facts	20
Glossary	22
To Learn More	23
Index	24

All About India

New Delhi

India is a **peninsula** in South Asia. Seas surround most sides of the country.

More than one billion people live in India! Its capital is New Delhi.

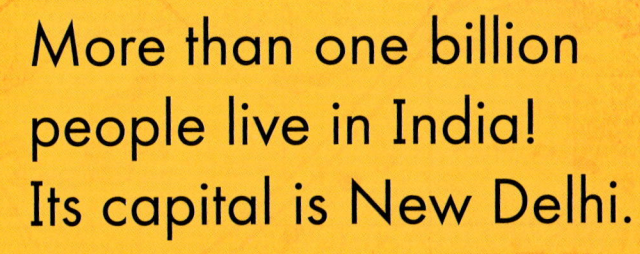

Land and Animals

India has many landscapes. The Himalayas is a mountain **range** in the north. The Ganges River flows nearby.

Plains cover central India. The Deccan **Plateau** is in the south.

Himalayas

Ganges River

Size: around 1,560 miles (2,510 kilometers) long

Famous For: important river in Hinduism

Monsoons drive India's **climate**. These winds change direction each season.

India has three seasons.
Springs are hot and dry.
Summers are hot and wet.
Winters are cool and dry.

Many animals call India home. Lions and tigers live in the south. Cows live on the plains.

cows

Quails run across the ground. Gharials eat fish in northern India.

Life in India

Indians come from many different backgrounds. Most practice **Hinduism**.

Hundreds of languages are spoken in India. Hindi is the most common.

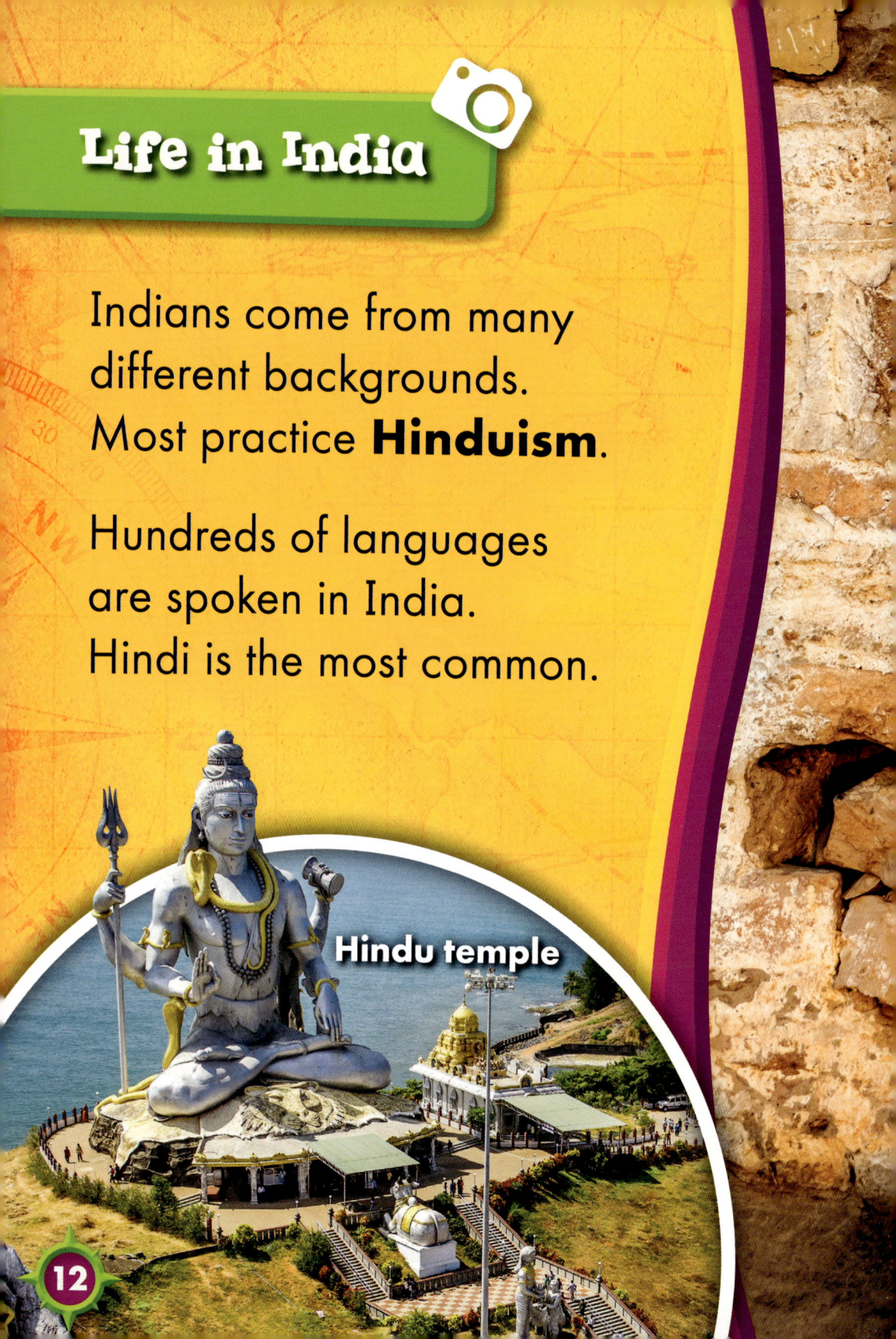

Hindu temple

Indians enjoy fun activities. Hiking and mountain climbing are popular. Rafting is also common.

Many Indians love cricket. Soccer is another popular sport.

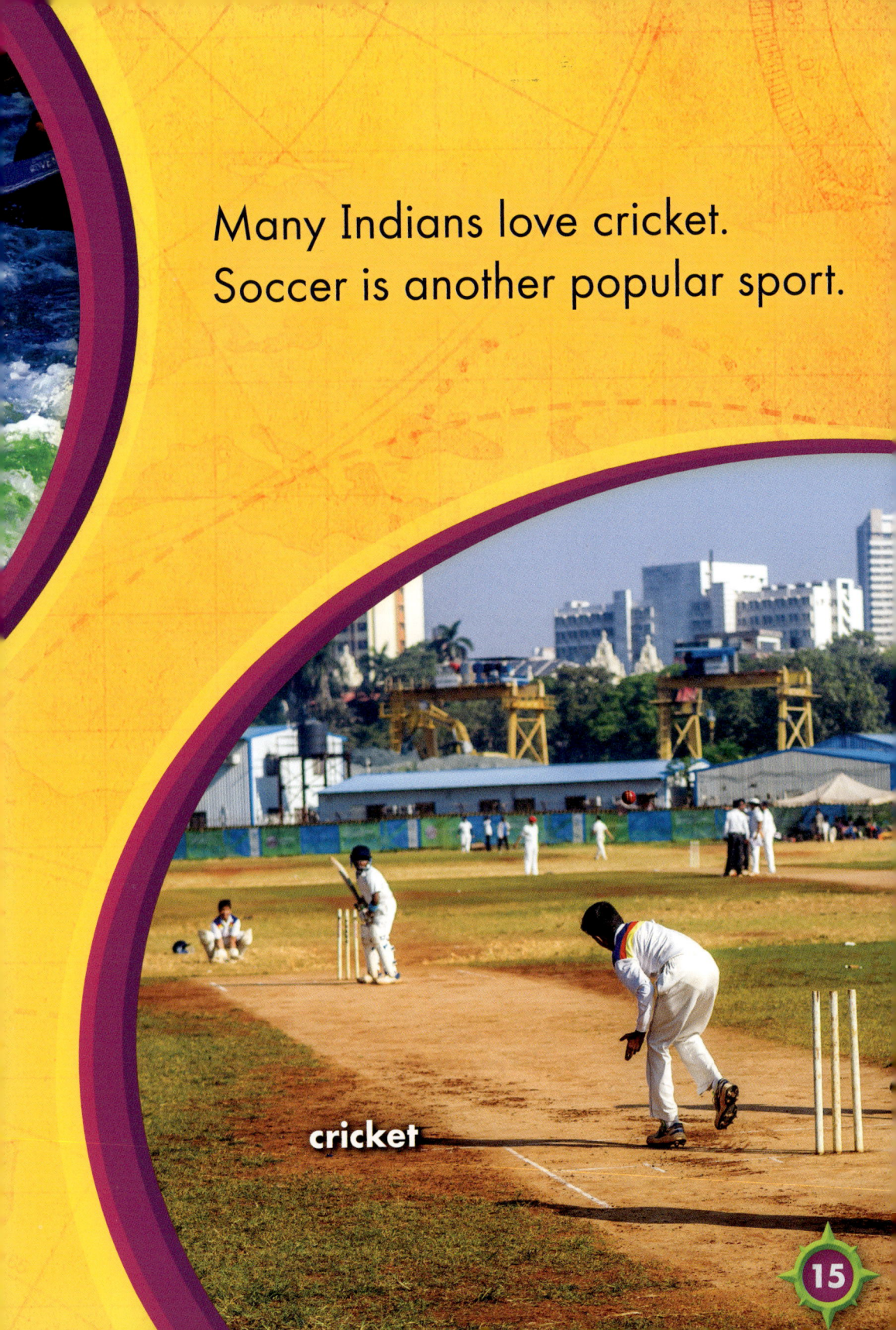

cricket

Rice and *chapati* are **staple** foods in India. They are often eaten with *dal*.

Biryani is a common rice dish. *Kheer* is a tasty pudding!

Indian Foods

chapati

dal

biryani

kheer

Holi

Many Indians **celebrate** Holi. This colorful **festival** is in spring.

Diwali is in the fall. Hindus light lamps and decorate their homes. India is full of celebration!

India Facts

Size:
1,269,219 square miles
(3,287,263 square kilometers)

Population:
1,389,637,446 (2022)

National Holiday:
Republic Day (January 26)

Main Languages:
Hindi, Bengali, Marathi

Capital City:
New Delhi

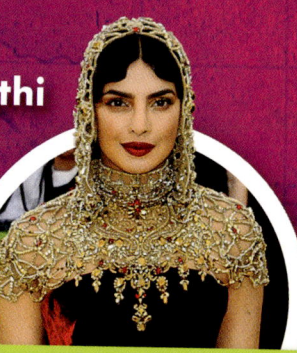

Famous Face

Name: Priyanka Chopra

Famous For: a model, singer, and actor

Religions

Muslim: 14%

other: 6%

Hindu: 80%

Top Landmarks

Qutub Minar

Swaminarayan Akshardham

Taj Mahal

Glossary

celebrate—to do something special or fun for a big event, occasion, or holiday

climate—the usual weather conditions in a certain place

festival—a time or event of celebration

Hinduism—a religion that began in India

monsoons—winds that shift direction each season; monsoons bring heavy rain.

peninsula—a section of land that extends out from a larger piece of land and is almost completely surrounded by water

plains—large areas of flat land

plateau—an area of raised, flat land

range—a group of mountains

staple—a widely used food or other item

To Learn More

AT THE LIBRARY

Grack, Rachel. *Holi*. Minneapolis, Minn.: Bellwether Media, 2019.

Mattern, Joanne. *India*. Minneapolis, Minn.: Pogo, 2019.

Soundararajan, Chitra. *Let's Look at India*. North Mankato, Minn.: Capstone, 2020.

ON THE WEB

FACTSURFER

Factsurfer.com gives you a safe, fun way to find more information.

1. Go to www.factsurfer.com.
2. Enter "India" into the search box and click 🔍.
3. Select your book cover to see a list of related content.

Index

animals, 10, 11
Asia, 4
capital (see New Delhi)
cricket, 15
Deccan Plateau, 6
Diwali, 19
foods, 16, 17
Ganges River, 6, 7
hiking, 14
Himalayas, 6
Hindi, 12, 13
Hinduism, 12, 19
Holi, 18
India facts, 20–21
map, 5
monsoons, 8

mountain climbing, 14
New Delhi, 4, 5
peninsula, 4
people, 5, 12
plains, 6, 10
rafting, 14
say hello, 13
seasons, 8, 9, 18, 19
soccer, 15

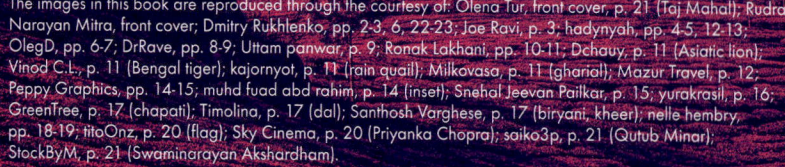

The images in this book are reproduced through the courtesy of: Olena Tur, front cover, p. 21 (Taj Mahal); Rudra Narayan Mitra, front cover; Dmitry Rukhlenko, pp. 2-3, 6, 22-23; Joe Ravi, p. 3; hadynyah, pp. 4-5, 12-13; OlegD, pp. 6-7; DrRave, pp. 8-9; Uttam panwar, p. 9; Ronak Lakhani, pp. 10-11; Dchauy, p. 11 (Asiatic lion); Vinod C.L., p. 11 (Bengal tiger); kajornyot, p. 11 (rain quail); Milkovasa, p. 11 (gharial); Mazur Travel, p. 12; Peppy Graphics, pp. 14-15; muhd fuad abd rahim, p. 14 (inset); Snehal Jeevan Pailkar, p. 15; yurakrasil, p. 16; GreenTree, p. 17 (chapati); Timolina, p. 17 (dal); Santhosh Varghese, p. 17 (biryani, kheer); nelle hembry, pp. 18-19; titoOnz, p. 20 (flag); Sky Cinema, p. 20 (Priyanka Chopra); saiko3p, p. 21 (Qutub Minar); StockByM, p. 21 (Swaminarayan Akshardham).